For Erin Bean
and Baby.
S.R.

For Katie, a
friendship story.
A.B.

OXFORD
UNIVERSITY PRESS

Great Clarendon Street, Oxford OX2 6DP

Oxford University Press is a department of the University of Oxford.
It furthers the University's objective of excellence in research, scholarship,
and education by publishing worldwide in

Oxford   New York

Auckland   Cape Town   Dar es Salaam   Hong Kong   Karachi
Kuala Lumpur   Madrid   Melbourne   Mexico City   Nairobi
New Delhi   Shanghai   Taipei   Toronto

With offices in
Argentina   Austria   Brazil   Chile   Czech Republic   France   Greece
Guatemala   Hungary   Italy   Japan   Poland   Portugal   Singapore
South Korea   Switzerland   Thailand   Turkey   Ukraine   Vietnam

Oxford is a registered trade mark of Oxford University Press
in the UK and in certain other countries

First published in 2011

British Library Cataloguing in Publication
Data available

ISBN: 978-0-19-278017-1 (hardback)
ISBN: 978-0-19-278018-8 (paperback)

10 9 8 7 6 5 4 3 2 1

Printed in China

Paper used in the production of this book is a
natural, recyclable product made from wood
grown in sustainable forests. The manufacturing
process conforms to the environmental
regulations of the country of origin.

I don't want to be a pea!

(The story of Hugo and Bella)

Ann Bonwill &
Simon Rickerty

OXFORD
UNIVERSITY PRESS

All hippos have birds,
and Bella is mine.

Correction.

All birds have hippos, and Hugo is mine.

Anyway. Where was I? Oh yes,
tonight is a very special night.

It is the
night of the

Hippo-Bird

Fairytale Fancy

Dress Party.

You mean the Bird-Hippo Fairytale Fancy Dress Party.

Whatever.

The important part is we have decided on a costume.

We are going to go dressed as the Princess and the Pea.

Don't we look lovely?

But I don't **want** to **be** a **pea**.

It is too **green** and **small.**

Instead I will be a . . .

How about a king and his jester?
You look smashing!

I
look
ri-dic-ulous.

We are **NOT**
going to be a king

and

his jester.

Let's try . . .

Cinderella and her pumpkin.

I will not be a pumpkin. Look how very orange I am.

I think you look
rather nice orange.

Thank you.
But I will still
not be a pumpkin.

It's getting late! We are going
to miss the party because of you.

If we miss the party,
it will be because of you.
You are the one who refused
to be a pea in the first place.

If you like peas so much,
then you can be the **pea**
and I will be the **princess.**

Besides, I don't even
want to go to the party
with you any more.

Well then, neither do I.

I've never been
to the Bird-Hippo
party without
Hugo.

Perhaps I could be a **pea** after all?

The party won't be
the same without Bella.

And she would make a
beautiful princess.

What a strange costume!
Who are you? **asks
a big bad hippo.**

And who
are YOU?
**asks
Little Red
Riding Bird.**

I am Hugo,
Bella's hippo.

I am Bella,
Hugo's bird.

And we're two peas in a pod . . .

just as it should be.